A. C. Allanby

THE TRANSOM TRILOGY II

THE END OF THE WORLD

Limited Special Edition. No. 9 of 25 Paperbacks

Angie Caroline Allanby is now well over 40 – but still young at heart. She works and lives in London with her family and an ever-growing menagerie. The whole family do love adventure, travel and the odd darts game – at which of course Angie always wins…

I would like to acknowledge the Men, Women and Children of our world who consciously choose to serve Goodness and Truth. This is a lonely journey, fraught with perils of misunderstanding, judgement and jealousy.

This work is dedicated to those who walk on this chosen path – unswayed by public opinion and with strong conviction in what they stand for.

Thank you, Most Excellent among Humanity.

Because of you, we progress.

A. C. Allanby

THE TRANSOM TRILOGY II

THE END OF THE WORLD

AUSTIN MACAULEY PUBLISHERS™
LONDON • CAMBRIDGE • NEW YORK • SHARJAH

Copyright © A. C. Allanby (2019)

The right of A. C. Allanby to be identified as author of this work has been asserted by her in accordance with section 77 and 78 of the Copyright, Designs and Patents Act 1988.

All rights reserved. No part of this publication may be reproduced, stored in a retrieval system, or transmitted in any form or by any means, electronic, mechanical, photocopying, recording, or otherwise, without the prior permission of the publishers.

Any person who commits any unauthorised act in relation to this publication, may be liable to criminal prosecution and civil claims for damages.

A CIP catalogue record for this title is available from the British Library.

ISBN 9781788237499 (Paperback)
ISBN 9781788237505 (Hardback)
ISBN 9781788237512 (Kindle e-book)
ISBN 9781528953771 (ePub e-book)

www.austinmacauley.com

First Published (2019)
Austin Macauley Publishers Ltd
25 Canada Square
Canary Wharf
London
E14 5LQ

Chapter 1
The Three Sisters of Orion

Celestial rocks pelted the three sisters, the Queens of Orion. As they raced through space, Angel and Genevieve formed a guard around Hannah and her fragile Star, just born. But the onslaught was becoming intense and they feared for the safety of the tiny new Princess.

This war was as ancient as space itself. In an effort to dominate the constellations and plunder their wealth, Durgon crushed any goodness in the heavens.

"Hannah, send her to safety. There is a guardian in another world. She will be safe there until she is strong and wise enough to return."

Genevieve's urgent whisper reached Hannah in their flight. The three shot through space at the speed of light, dodging asteroids.

Hannah knew that Genevieve was right. With Star Princess safe, the three sisters could fight and preserve her future. She WAS the future.

There was no time to lose. Durgon's meteors were catching up and his spies already knew of the tiny Star's existence. They would not stop until she was destroyed.

Angel gently placed the Princess in a crystal bottle. As light swirled and enfolded them, the three sisters held the bottle suspended between them, as if therein held their own hearts. Pure love burned intensely blue, so bright that light years away all the stars turned towards the glow. A tiny new born, beautiful and fragile star glowed and hovered inside.

"Be safe! Be strong! We will come for you, Star of my heart!" cried Hannah. And with that, the three sisters flung the bottle with all their celestial might and the unlikely cocoon flew like a tiny shooting star through darkness and space, just in time.

Suddenly, they were pelted with meteors. Hannah spiralled out of control, her light veil ripped and shredded. Angel floated away stunned by a meteor hit, while Genevieve shot asteroids back to protect her constellation.

The battle did not last long. The three sisters were battered. Scorpio and Aquarius whisked them away and hid the three in the deepest reaches of space—far away from Durgon's spies—until they recovered and could again take up their position as Orion's Belt.

***

The tiny bottle, holding what looked like a grain of sand, tumbled through the clouds of another world and landed with a splash in a vast ocean. The bottle floated undisturbed through currents and eddies, nosed by sharks and spun along in the wake of whales, was tossed in the air by playful dolphins, and thrown up and down by stormy waves. Huge battle galleons swished past, brushing the tiny star aside in their haste and great monsters from the Deep fought beneath as the bottle bobbed by.

Yet, the little bottle continued unharmed through the passage of time. Galleons gave way to clippers, merchant vessels crossed its path and once a huge awkward three winged aeroplane flew right over. Through seasons and wars, the bottle bobbed and twirled and stayed safe.

Then one day, the tiny bottle was blown by the wind and washed by the current down a whirlpool tunnel to rest on a white shell-strewn beach.

A group of children came running along the beach. Several young girls collected cowrie shells in their woven baskets, while a gang of boisterous boys waded in the rock pools finding oysters and popping them in their sling bags.

An energetic lad found the little bottle. He knew not that he held in his palm the future of Orion. As the warmth of his hand heated the tiny star, the grain began to glow.

The star was awakening. The grain shone brighter and brighter, and started to jump. As the boy looked closer, the star leapt and bounced inside the bottle. Maybe this was a firefly that wanted to get out, thought the boy.

Without a second thought, the boy held the little bottle high and with a SMASH, shattered the crystal on a rock. The tiny star tumbled out onto the shells. The boy reached down to pick up the glowing grain but before he could, he was thrown back by a brilliant explosion of yellow starlight.

The children dropped their bags and baskets and fled in fright. They ran as fast as their legs could carry them back to their nearby village to tell their exciting tale.

Where the glowing grain had landed amongst the shells, there now lay a very little girl. She was curled up as if sleeping, her face tucked into her knees and dark curls blowing in the gentle breeze. The tiny girl stirred and stretched, and rubbed her little face, as if after a very long and very deep sleep. But when she opened her eyes they glowed—gently at first, and then they brightened—and suddenly like a flash shot light and sparkles all the way down the shell beach and across the bay. She stood—a bit wobbly at first—and played happily in the surf and sand, and rock pools. Then she made her way into the jungle.

Before long, the Shining Girl began to explore the World of the Whirlpool tunnel. She stopped when tired and slept in tree roots. She bathed in fresh bubbling streams and ate off the bounty of the jungle. She giggled at the birds and butterflies, and chased rabbits, played with sticks and made herself a leafy crown. And for a while, she was truly happy in this strange and beautiful world.

Then one day, with eyes shining, she crossed a wagon track and upon that wagon track was, at that moment riding, the meanest and largest of all tavern owners. The little Shining Girl was taken by that mean man and held prisoner, and he used her starlight gifts for his own gain—the task of infusing his beer with a sparkle that made his tavern very famous indeed.

That is, until Captain Antonio, Land and Sea happened upon the Rickety Mast Tavern in search of a liquorice lifeboat for their schooner '*Transom*' and rescued the Shining Girl, Star Princess. They had no idea that they had become the guardians of a treasure more precious than they could ever imagine.

***

Hannah awoke! She knew that the time would come when the three sisters would bring Star Princess home to her rightful place. But for now, Hannah, Genevieve and Angel needed rest to recover their strength and to join forces with those who stood for Goodness and Truth in the heavens.

Until then, they were content that their future constellation was safe, on board a special ship with a very special crew.

Chapter 2
The Storm

Captain Antonio was worried.
'*Transom*' was held in the grip of a storm that was worse than the one in which he lost '*Little Nook*' a long time ago. What was left of '*Transom*'s' splintered bowsprit plunged deep into huge walls of water as waves exploded over her deck. She pitched up and then violently down to smack each new towering wave with a bone-crunching jar. Her stern mast was snapped in half, and the half that had broken off was lost in the boiling waves after punching a hole in the deck and ripping away all of the rigging lines.

'*Transom*', loyal and strong as she was, merely took the pounding bravely and carried on. She did not really mind what happened to her, but at all costs she knew that she must keep her crew safe.

The crew were also in an interesting mix of a right mess, except for the youngest member. Roly Poly giggled and rolled to and fro quite happily on the galley floor, knowing that he was safe with '*Transom*'. He did not seem to notice the screaming of the wind or the tearing of the sails off the booms.

Max was mostly occupied with trying to keep all four of his legs underneath him while making sure the Captain had a good grip on the ship's wheel. The Great Dog was not at all sure how or whom he would try to save if '*Transom*' went down. So each time a bright fork of lightning speared the ocean, Max yelped and sat quivering on his tail, one miserable wet ear draped over his eyes. But even Captain Antonio ordering him below decks would not make him budge from the Captain's side, and so the two were worried and drenched through together.

The Explorers, strapping young lads Land and Sea, were busy getting tangled in all sorts of debris on '*Transom*'s' bucking deck. They were supposed to be tying off ropes and securing sails that had come loose—if they could only get there. Shreds of fabric from ripped sails, whipped in the wind and wet with stinging saltwater, slapped them both silly, until they gave up fighting the pitching deck and flying ropes. They sat in a dejected heap with feet braced against the rails and heads tucked down, wishing with all their hearts that the storm would pass.

La Chocolat staggered all through the cabins and back again, plugging leaks and noting repairs for after. She stowed everything she could find in safe places, so that nobody would be hurt by flying knives and pots, or toothbrushes and potatoes, or by the secret stash of the Captain's chocolate and rum for that matter. La Chocolat, now that she knew where the secret stash was kept—thanks to the storm—remained loyally silent on the subject and has never told a soul.

The seagulls, Pip and Lotta, had burrowed their way deep inside the lifejacket locker and so were warm, safe and dry, but their home in the crow's nest had gone overboard with the mast. Pip was particularly concerned because he had a very important message to deliver. Captain Antonio that very day had had a long chat with the talking seagull, and they finally decided upon the fate of La Chocolat. Antonio did not write to inform the Chocolate Ambassador that his daughter was safe as he was sure the message would be intercepted by the Evil Emperor's spies, placing her—and himself—back in danger. After Pip had assured the Captain that the Chocolate Ambassador and his wife were truly good and true, the brave seagull had promised to take the news of their daughter's rescue to them himself, and was charged with the delivery of an invitation for them to visit the schooner as soon as she docked again in her home port. It was important that La Chocolat's family know of her safety.

Through a big saloon porthole, Star Princess was watching huge green waves crashing over '*Transom*'. With each angry churning swell, she lisp-yelled, "Here comth another one!" At which, La Chocolat would brace herself, Roly would prepare for another trip across the saloon, and Star would tuck in her head, grip the porthole tight and wait for '*Transom*' to be pounded again. Both of the little girls were fairly frightened but each time Star was ready to burst into tears, La Chocolat somehow knew and shouted, "It's okay, the Captain and Max are still at the helm!" And each time La Chocolat was too exhausted to carry on, Roly Poly would explode in a particularly crazy chuckle and her spirits would lift.

Ship and crew were, frankly, battered, exhausted and scared.

'*Transom*' was en route to Bear de Sol with sand soap. A tall ship had been wrecked on their beaches in the same storms that now threatened '*Transom*' and the tall ship had been carrying a cargo of jelly. The jelly had washed ashore and set on the lovely de Sol sands and so instead of glistening white beaches, Bear de Sol now sported sticky cherry, lime, blackcurrant and lemon streaks. The Mayor had asked the first available ship to bring him sand soap to restore the beauty of their beaches. And so '*Transom*' found herself loaded and on her way quicker than you could get your hat and shoes to go out on a fine day.

Captain Antonio thought many thoughts in those stormy hours, '*Banjo*' tossing nervously behind him in her stays. He thought of his crew, all of whom depended on him. He thought of beautiful '*Transom*' and '*Banjo*', whom he loved with all of his big heart. He was glad Mermaid Marguerite was not sailing with them. She was right now translating Mer to the Humanitarian Society of All Ocean Creatures (Mer language did not really need translating to the Society, but as with most committees filled with old men they needed a pretty young thing to help along the right decisions).

And so, Captain Antonio prayed, as he had in that terrible storm before he was thrown from '*Little Nook*' and after which his life had been saved:

"Dear God, if you are there, and if you live, and if you care for us, please bring us through this storm. Protect those I love more than my own life. Amen."

The Captain's heart grew calm and for the first time in some hours, he was able to smile at Max and rough up the fur around his neck. Max knew then that they would be safe and that the Captain knew it too, so he let out one victorious bark for all the crew to hear.

Land and Sea heard Max, their eyes met, and they struggled to their feet. With new energy, they battled up and put their backs to their work. La Chocolat heard Max and she stopped what she was doing for a moment and smiled right down to her toes. Star heard Max and let go of her porthole to clap her hands in glee—just as another huge wave broke over '*Transom*' and she found herself rolling on the floor next to a chuckling Roly. Roly heard Max and let loose with a long gurgling giggle. The seagulls heard Max and Pip let out a rather large coo of relief.

And so, before Captain Antonio could wipe the next sheet of water from his face, La Chocolat swayed before him with a flask of coffee. Star Princess followed her up through the hatch, climbing unsteadily with thick slabs of nut cake in her tiny backpack.

The Captain tapped Max on the rump and sent him down to check on Roly. He really wanted the Great Dog to dry out as humans can easily change their soaking clothes, but drying dripping fur is somewhat harder, and Max was starting to shiver. Captain Antonio whistled a signal up to Land and Sea, who stumbled back to the cockpit where they collapsed after a good job done. All ropes were stowed and the damaged sail was secured on the boom to be attended to on a calmer ocean. They had also secured a thick canvas over the hole in the deck.

The Explorers shooed the Captain and girls down the hatch. After sharing quick sips from the warm flask, Land and Sea set the helm to keep the ship straight on her course and went below to get warm and dry. There they locked 'Transom' up tight, changed all of their wet oilskins and snuggled under warm blankets, which they piled on the Captain too. But he was already fast asleep, his chin sunk to his chest, their fate given over to a Mightier Hand.

Land and Sea both fully intended to stay on watch, but as each lad grew warmer, their eyes grew heavier... and heavier... and closed...

And while 'Transom's' crew slept, the full moon sent probes of silver light through the menacing clouds to splash upon her deck. The silver splashes grew and spread, and in the storm a deep rumble that was not thunder, echoed. Radiating out from 'Transom', the waves began to lose their wild anger, and the wind stopped screaming and began to sigh. The rain became fresh torrents of water instead of angry freezing needles, and eventually the torrents changed to soft fat drops. And all the while that the light danced and worked, the crew slept and dreamed.

***

The Captain awoke to a crystal clear morning sun shining through the portholes. He jumped to his feet to race on deck.

La Chocolat beat him to the hatch and calmly handed him a hot mug of coffee. "It's okay Captain. Land and Sea are top side," she said, smiling widely.

"Whew! Good lads!" exclaimed Antonio with relief. He took the coffee, planted a kiss on La Chocolat's curly head in thanks and then looked around to see that everyone was unharmed.

Roly and Max snored on while the girls tinkered in the galley, finding the odd item wedged firmly in the most unexpected places—like the salt cellar in the roof and the ocean charts in the pantry. The Captain finished his coffee quickly and made his cautious way on deck.

The ocean shone like diamonds in all directions, calm as a sheet of glass. The whole ship glistened so brightly that he put up a hand to shield his eyes. Land and Sea worked diligently changing the shredded foresail and clearing the deck of splinters.

The Captain knew from the tingling in his toes that a Mighty Force had been busy here. His heart filled with thanks and rubbing his hands together in glee, he declared, "Hey doggies! It's a miracle! We still float!"

Land and Sea laughed with him, and then a flock of seagulls found them. Very soon, Max was chasing gulls, the girls were frying breakfast, the Explorers set to discussing where they would adventure first in this new destination and Roly Poly was giving the Captain instructions from the dolphins on the best way to get through the rocks leading to the port. Pip and Lotta were gliding merrily overhead, catching up with their species on any tweets they had missed on their voyage.

And Captain Antonio?

He had toe-tingling, finger-tapping excitement bubbling in his chest and so as they neared port he broke into song:

"Tumdedumdum, it's a BOTTLE O' RUM FOR ME!"

Chapter 3
The Stranded Sailors of Bear De Sol

'*Transom*' sailed slowly towards Bear de Sol on one tattered sail. She was looking a lot worse for wear and not at all like her usual graceful self after the storm. But the ship and all of her crew buzzed eagerly. As '*Transom*' drifted into the harbour, her crew surveyed the port in great surprise.

The docks were crammed with boats of all sizes. All of them were in varied degrees of disrepair so that the harbour looked like a wreckage yard. And about the harbour was an air of hopeless silence that seemed strange compared with the excited activity on board the schooner. The Explorers shrugged and got back to work; the girls frowned at each other and got back to work; Max, Roly and Antonio stood together on the bow, but did not get back to work. The whole situation of this still harbour was rather puzzling.

After mooring, their first job was to find a shipbuilder from whom they could buy a new mast and bowsprit, and a sail maker where they could get new sails. Captain Antonio and the Explorers set off on their quest, leaving the girls, Roly and Max on board, hard at work clearing the mess of broken debris and splinters, knotted ropes and wet everything.

After a short walk, they found exactly what they were looking for. The street leading out of the harbour was lined on both sides by many different shipbuilders. The three sailors entered, first one, then the next and the next, looking for what they needed. By the time they had got to the end of the road, the Captain was beginning to feel somewhat disheartened.

Each mast cost far more than the Captain knew they were worth. The sails were very expensive and what they were charging for white oak to repair the deck was downright criminal. As for the repair men themselves, they were a rude lot of louts.

Captain Antonio shook his head and returned to '*Transom*' and see what they could save in the wreckage on board. Land and Sea still wanted to explore further, so the two lads continued on.

Captain Antonio was rather depressed when he arrived back on board the schooner. He climbed down the hatch slowly, feeling suddenly old and tired. Star Princess immediately cuddled in his lap and La Chocolat sat by him while he told them the news.

"Don't worry Cappy, something will happen," said an irrepressible Roly from his perch on Max's back. Roly had discovered that Max's ears were perfect handholds for a good gallop. No one knew what Max felt about this arrangement, as with his ears pulled back, his mouth smiled hugely whether he wanted to or not.

They sat quietly together for a moment. Presently, La Chocolat slipped out and returned with a small wooden box, her brown eyes big beneath her spiral curls.

"Maybe this can help us," she said as she handed the box over to Captain Antonio. The Captain opened up the lid and smiled down to his toes at her thoughtfulness.

Inside, the little box was full to the top with spiral strands of pure red gold.

At that moment, the Explorers burst through the hatch in agonies of excitement.

"Captain, Captain, we found us a mast! It's a beauty! All we need to do is chop down a tree!" exploded Land. Sea was busy doing some version of a victory dance and of course was joined by Star. Their infectious laughter soon had everyone asking a hundred questions all at once.

Captain Antonio put his hands up in surrender. "What would I do without you skellem lot, I ask you? Now, let's go and see this mast for ourselves. Lads, bring what tools you need!" As the crew prepared to go ashore, Antonio locked away the precious little box of gold, still shaking his head in amazement. He did slap his thigh several times and was heard to mumble, "Thunder and lightning!", as they all raced backwards and forwards to cabins, holds and lockers to find the tools they needed and batten the ship so they could go ashore.

Star rode on the Captain's shoulders, Roly on Max's back, and they were off.

The Explorers soon had the crew following a trail out of town. As they topped a gentle hill, they gazed over the ridge and beheld gloriously tall and beautifully strong gum trees as far as their eye could see. A young man and a pretty lady sat waiting for them in the shade of the trees and welcomed them warmly.

"Any way we can be of help, please let us know," said the young man, who introduced himself as the forester and the pretty lady as his wife, who was the local nurse, school teacher and seamstress. "We don't have a lot, but what we have we gladly give to you to help in your misfortune."

Land led the Captain to a fine gum close to the road that would slot perfectly into '*Transom*'s' masthead. While the forester and Sea got busy felling the tall gum tree, Land prepared to plant another tree, because as you well know, that is how things should be done. The others returned to town to visit the Mayor about their cargo.

Before nightfall, the crew met back on '*Transom*'. The Captain had asked some of the other deckhands around the harbour to help with carrying their new mast back to their ship, and the felled trunk lay on the dock ready for new sails and rigging to be fitted.

"With our payment for the cargo, our new mast and La Chocolat's gold we will be setting sail soon," the Captain said that night while the crew shared delicious stew and dumplings. "We must ask the forester's wife if she can make sails."

As they were finishing dinner, there was a sharp rap on the rail and a deep voice bellowed, "Permission to come aboard!"

Sea poked his head out of the hatch and let out a low whistle. "What's this then gents?" he said a little worriedly, for the dock was crowded with the sailors from the other yachts.

Captain Antonio and his crew then sat on the deck, as the sailors told them the story of how they had all limped into harbour after terrible storms over the past six full moons. But none of them had been able to afford the services of the ruthless ship repair men. So time had come and gone, and forgotten them there—unable to sail onward and unable to carry out repairs. They were hopeless and they missed their families.

The *'Transom'* sailors looked at each other. Of course, they could not hear of troubles and not do something to solve the problem. So Captain Antonio stood up slowly, and after a moment's thought he spoke, "When I sail from this harbour you will all sail with me, in your own vessels in good repair. So let's get to work already!"

A cheer rose from the crowd and through that long night, they made lists of repairs for each of the yachts. They all took turns making lots of cups of strong coffee that kept them alert and thinking cleverly, and Sea whipped up a big batch of muffins right when the coffee was not working anymore. Eventually, they all yawned and curled up in their bunks, just when midnight turned to morning. Captain Antonio, however, did not sleep. He sat at *'Transom'*'s' chart table and went through each list for each yacht, wrote long, long lists and generally put his brain to work properly to find a solution as quickly as possible for the stranded sailors.

As dawn broke and sparkled on the de Sol sands that were now clean (thanks to *'Transom'*, whose cargo the Mayor had put to immediate use), hope filled the air of the port for the first time in months. The men all stood ready with tools and the Captain with his instructions. He despatched a team of sailors to the forest with Land in charge, to the Mayor with Sea in charge and to the seamstress with La Chocolat in charge. Captain Antonio wanted to visit the shipbuilders' yards himself and give those ruthless profiteers a piece of his mind. Only *'Transom'*'s crew knew what that meant.

And sure enough the sky soon grew dark. All creatures scurried for shelter and cowered in terror, and the very earth shook with a violent tremor. A great roar of rage thundered over the earth; the ocean echoed with a distant, "Boom boom! Boom boom!"

And '*Transom*'s' crew knew that those crooked shipbuilders would no longer be in any shape to do any more crookery.

For many days, the sailors all worked and sang together under the '*Transom*' crews' direction. One by one, each yacht was declared seaworthy again. The shipbuilders were put out of business once and for all by the Mayor, and the very happy forester and his wife were put in charge of the port and all ship repairs. '*Transom*' looked breath-taking with a brand new set of turquoise sails made by the forester's wife, painted around the edges with shells, fish, coral and waves, resting on strong new booms. A fine new bowsprit pointed straight and true, and a new mast stood high and proud against blue skies. And the Captain declared that it was time for them to set sail.

As each ship prepared to leave, the harbour was abuzz with joyful activity. One Captain was returning to meet his newborn son after leaving his wife newly pregnant, and he approached '*Transom*'s' Captain respectfully.

"Only you have made this possible, sir. I thank you from the bottom of my heart, and I give you all I have." With that, he emptied his money bag into Star's apron, and turned on his heel back to his ship. There followed after him every sailor. Some gave gold and others a silver coin or two. Some gave a fish, then there arrived two large, richly orange pumpkins, a packet of fragrant spices from the east and a lovely intricately carved walrus tusk. But all of the sailors had one thing in common: each would be loyal friends of '*Transom*' and her crew forever more.

And so, the fleet of ships that sailed from Bear de Sol has never since been matched, and the full moon that they left in was calm, and happy, and free.

Chapter 4
The Chocolate Ambassador's Family

'*Transom*' was anchored at her home port and her crew sat upon deck. Each had a piece of rope and Captain Antonio was teaching them how to tie a bowline. Max managed to knot his rope around two paws and his nose, and Roly Poly lay back against the mast giggling helplessly at the Great Dog. Star Princess held loops of rope wound into flower petals as she sang happily. Sea threaded a hook through one end of his rope and was throwing this overboard to try and catch a fish. The Captain shook his head and rolled his eyes. He was not getting very far in this important lesson. Only Land and La Chocolat were making progress.

At that moment, the postman arrived. The postman was a cheery old man, whom the crew secretly believed was Father Christmas. Up they all jumped, except Max who yelped a muffled yelp and sat up on his hind legs with his front paws tied firmly to his snout.

"How's my favourite crew?" yelled the postman, and swung easily on board with a big mail sack slung on his back. While he opened the sack and began passing letters to the Captain, he asked, "Been anywhere interesting?"

He gave La Chocolat a fat envelope while she told him of the Ocean Kelp Jungle of Banoon and how the dolphins had to pull them through it.

Land said, "I think the most interesting place we have been recently is to the Ice Kingdom. Everything we ate was made of ice but tasted exactly like what it was meant to be. We had a LOT of brain freeze, though."

Star found the geyser escalators the best because she loved the way '*Transom*' chuckled when the geysers threw the ship in the air, and '*Transom*' was shot up higher and higher until they reached the Ocean of the Clouds. The cargo they had carried there was bubble-gum cloud flavouring which tasted terrible, but when mixed with the right kind of cloud—thick and misty, and not too grey—you would think you had tasted heaven.

Captain Antonio made an announcement, as he opened the most important looking message first. "Mermaid Marguerite will be joining us on our next voyage! She sent an eel mail!"

Shouts and whoops filled the air. Using their ropes as lassoes, the Explorers chased each other around the deck.

Meanwhile, La Chocolat was bouncing with excitement while reading her letter. Captain Antonio also had a letter from the Mayor of Alkalone that he wanted to show her. And so, after saying goodbye to the postman who was busy untying a mournful Max, he sat down beside her. He quietly told her some news, and La Chocolat's eyes got very big and she covered her open mouth with her hand. Captain Antonio smiled widely, and their eyes danced with fabulous secrets. They both looked over to where Roly Poly was playing.

Now if you recall correctly, the Mayor of Alkalone was so pleased with '*Transom*'s' delivery of grape seedlings, that he had promised Antonio he would assist in finding the parents of Roly Poly. The Mayor was a very clever man, and so had quietly gone about that errand with diligence and perseverance.

After reading La Chocolat's letter—with some difficulty as the letter was all in French and La Chocolat had been teaching the crew to speak her language—Captain Antonio slapped his thigh. "Well well, Marguerite is not the only one who will be visiting. We must swab the decks and cook up some good food. La Chocolat's family is coming to meet us!"

And with that, the Captain winked at her, and they smiled happily at each other. They had another good reason of their own to be excited about this visit.

Captain Antonio was a little worried that La Chocolat's family would want to take her home, and he knew they would all miss her very, very much. And if the news he had just received from the Mayor of Alkalone proved to be correct, then things would definitely change on board.

So '*Transom*' was again alive with buzzing activity, each of her crew cheerfully occupied—if somewhat apprehensively in the Captain's case—preparing fine food and comfortable berths for their guests.

They were all busy about their tasks when a lovely tune filled the air. Only one person they knew in the whole world could sing quite like that. They all dropped what they were doing, and ran down the ship and up the ship, and down masts and up from cabins to the stern where the beautiful Mermaid Marguerite was boarding. The joy of seeing her again and her seeing them again made them all quite silly. Marguerite's anemone silk skirt floated around her legs, her hair was done in tiny braids with ocean diamond clasps and around her head she wore a coral-flower tiara. A squeak from the water called her attention back, and they all looked overboard to see a dolphin holding a little woven sea kelp bag in her beak which she threw playfully to the Captain and soaked him nicely in the process. They all laughed, and the Mermaid Princess's swordfish bodyguards disappeared with the dolphin into the green harbour depths.

They did not have long to wait after that for the family of La Chocolat to find '*Transom*'. The girls cooked happily with Marguerite while Roly and Max were busy making a nest with all of the rope from their earlier lesson. The Explorers were sword fighting with baguettes after scrubbing the deck and polishing the brass. Captain Antonio was inspecting '*Transom*' with a critical eye to make sure all was in ship shape order, when there was a clipping of hooves on the dock and the dinkiest carriage ever stopped next to the ship. A carriage door opened and out stepped the Chocolate Ambassador followed by his very lovely wife.

He was the colour of shining ebony cocoa and his wife looked like a dreamy white chocolate figurine. They were both dressed in lovely regal satin robes that swished gently. In her gloved hands, the Chocolate Ambassador's wife held a box of truffles that she handed with a graceful curtsey to the Captain. Then she stepped on board, took her daughter in her arms and squeezed her until the crew were sure she would burst! The Chocolate Ambassador followed his wife more shyly and placed a very heartfelt kiss on top of La Chocolat's soft spiral curls and whispered, "Ma Cherie! Merci Dieu, merci!"

Over glasses of thick hot chocolate and rum, the Chocolate Ambassador and his wife laughed and cried over the re-telling of their daughter's adventures and her rescue by the Captain.

But eventually the Ambassador's wife had to tell them. "We very much would like to have our daughter at home," she said quietly.

The Captain looked down into his glass. Max put a paw on his knee and yelped a compassionate whimper. The Explorers' smiles faded and became frowns of disbelief. Star immediately burst into tears. But then, the wife added, "However, when I told my very good friend Marguerite of our wish for La Chocolat to come home, she made a fine suggestion that we must consider for the future of chocolate everywhere." Here she turned to her husband, who sat forward to speak.

"The Mer people do not know of chocolate at all," he said sadly. "Marguerite has come up with an answer to this tragedy. She proposed that La Chocolat stay on board '*Transom*' to be a Chocolate Ambassador to the Mer. If our daughter can bring chocolate to the ocean people, we can meet her in ports with more supplies of cocoa and candy whenever she needs. Marguerite tells us that '*Transom*' is a well-respected vessel among the Mer and so if you are willing Captain Antonio, and La Chocolat if you would like to stay on board, this will be a worthy task."

At that, Marguerite handed her woven kelp bag to the Chocolate Ambassador. Inside was a Royal Seal Scroll with an official request from the Ocean King himself, for chocolate to be sent to his people.

Well, the Captain's eyes could not have gotten any bigger. He glanced in amazement at Marguerite, who grinned happily back, and then he smiled at La Chocolat. "You know how we feel. We would be lost without you. Would you consider staying on board with us and spreading chocolate to all Mer, even to the deepest depths of the Greatest Ocean?"

Land and Sea looked at each other with glee. To carry chocolate all over the world? What could be better! "La Chocolat, we vote you stay and bring chocolate along for us too!" voted Sea punching the air, and they all laughed.

La Chocolat thought for a long, long moment. Everybody held their breaths… At last she said, "Papa, I would love to help you with your work more than anything. I would feel honoured to be entrusted with such an important task. And I would love to stay on board '*Transom*'. And so I accept!"

'*Transom*'s' crew all heaved sighs of relief, and La Chocolat's parents beamed proudly. But La Chocolat held up her hand for silence.

"But I have a question for you now." With that she looked at Captain Antonio, who nodded quickly, so she went across to Roly who was helping Max devour a stolen baguette. La Chocolat lifted the little boy and carried him across to her parents, wriggling and giggling in her arms.

"This is Roly Poly. He speaks Fish. Captain Antonio has been trying to find his parents with the help of the Mayor of Alkalone and we received word just today." Here she paused and glanced at the Captain who nodded reassuringly. "Is it possible that he could be my brother?"

The Chocolate Ambassador gasped and his wife's eyes filled with tears, as they looked at each other in astonishment. "C-could this be? Our baby son was stolen from us at Afireesha. We have not ever stopped searching for him these past three years," said the wife as La Chocolat handed Roly to her. "Yes. This is my son…" and she dissolved in tears and squeezed him until his eyes nearly popped out.

And so, this unexpected visit became a touching and very lovely family reunion. Roly giggled delightedly as he was cuddled and loved, and tickled and kissed. Tears flowed and heartfelt thanks spoken, and more stories were told. Antonio decided that the Chocolate Ambassador and his wife should sail with them on their next voyage.

Early the following morning found a supply of toffee and fudge in cocoa wrapping being nestled on board the schooner for delivery to the Great Ocean King. She also carried a cargo of cedar wood ordered by the Lord of Langs, and so '*Transom*' had a tide to catch. But never had she carried such a happy crew—possibly the happiest that the world had ever seen!

And so as '*Transom*'s' sails lifted to the wind, her crew took into their hearts the family of their well-loved La Chocolat and Roly Poly, and they knew that all was right with the world when a lost son comes home.

Chapter 5
Memories

If you were to have taken an evening walk after a certain lovely day in late autumn, and happened to stroll down to the harbour, and if that harbour just so happened to be the home port of the graceful schooner '*Transom*', you might just have been lucky enough to peek through that ship's porthole or down her open hatch, and witness a scene that you would love to be part of.

For on board was a special night. After sharing a particularly delicious dinner cooked up by La Chocolat and Sea that involved all of the crew's favourite foods, Land voted that they play Favourite Adventure Charades. Dishes were cleared and washed pronto, glasses of warm milk with cinnamon and honey handed out and a box of tendernut truffles passed around.

Then the fun began.

Captain Antonio went first. Giving an elaborate bow, he swept his imaginary hat off his head and blew kisses to all the crew. Star collapsed laughing, Roly and Max howled in disgust, the Explorers wolf whistled and La Chocolat blushed. Of course Antonio's favourite adventure was when he delivered the Lady of Neshev and her six beautiful daughters their summer wardrobe without a single salt water stain, and they all came down to the docks and kissed Antonio on both cheeks to thank him. Nobody needed to be very clever to guess that one.

Roly jumped up next. He pushed himself like an inch worm all across the floor, and then leapt up onto the table, bellowing and roaring with hands whirring like a windmill. To shouts of "Very good!" and "Not bad acting!" he giggled and snorted and waddled his chubby middle.

"Definitely the Monsters of the Tropic Eclipse," said Sea, and so he was up next.

Sea took his post and thought for a minute. Then he walked to and fro, stopping and looking confused before changing course and retracing steps. He put his hand to his head and frowned terribly. Then he turned circles and chewed a fingernail. La Chocolat jumped up and down.

"The Forgetful Ocean! The Forgetful Ocean, I bet you!" she yelled, and everyone burst out laughing. Of course! The ocean upon which she had forgotten to salt the porridge every day for a month, the Captain had forgotten to shave for so long that he had grown a beard down to his middle, the Explorers forgot how to tie knots and so had nearly lost '*Banjo*', Max forgot to eat, and Roly forgot who he was. Only Star had kept her wits and all she forgot was how to tell the time—which she still has not remembered to this day.

"You're up," Sea said to La Chocolat, and flopped on the saloon rug to enjoy his truffle. La Chocolat took the stage rather shyly, but she did not need to think of her favourite. That was easy.

She waved her arms fluidly about her, and swayed like a young tree in the wind. Then she lurched about the saloon like a drunken sailor, but gracefully—only La Chocolat could still be graceful while acting a not so elegant memory. Star was jumping on the seat yelling lisp-fully, "The mermaid dantherth at Mendor!"

The crew collapsed laughing again. Captain Antonio looked sheepish. At the Great Meeting of the Human and Mer People held at Mendor, he had given the mermaid dancers a bottle of champagne. He was not to know, however, that the Mer people and champagne do not mix like humans and champagne. The dance by the dizzy troop that had followed had sent sprays of salt water all over the decorated ships and drenched the Cardinal and his wife in their finery. While the '*Transom*' crew had doubled over in laughter, they realised that the Cardinal did not have a very good sense of humour. The Great Ocean King had saved the day, and offered the

Cardinal a draught of Giggle Spice. After that the event was thankfully a success.

So Star's turn came next. She shuffled her way to the stage on her knees, humming and thinking. Then she curled up into a tiny ball and was very still. Slowly, one finger emerged from the ball and then a little hand, followed by an arm. Her fingers wriggled, and then she followed her outstretched arm, until Star was standing straight up with her tiny hands reaching high for the deck above. Then she slowly crumpled back into a ball again.

Land whistled. "Wow, Star, that was fabulous! The tree-eggs in the Ocean of Nothing. Remember the eggs we found on deck, and each night they hatched into tall fruit trees, and each morning they were eggs again. Without those tree-eggs we would have starved. The fruit they bore each night fed us after the flocks of birds kept raiding us during the days."

"Yes, and when we arrived at Trigold they disappeared into thin air. No other sailor has ever seen them. They are supposed to be mythical gifts from the stars to the Guardians of Earth," the Captain added thoughtfully.

Land hopped up. "There was nothing mythical about THAT fruit. And now I am going to teach you little ones some '*Transom*' history," he laughed.

And so he squatted on one knee and scratched at the timbers beneath him. His face was twisted into a very mean scowl and he looked around at each of the crew growling and grunting. Suddenly, he went sprawling across the floor as if he had been kicked. Then he scurried around as if he was being chased. Everyone was shouting with laughter, the girls had tears of mirth rolling down their cheeks, but only the Captain and Sea knew which adventure Land was remembering.

"Land, you picked a good one," laughed the Captain, "but I get to tell the story this time."

The crew settled down to listen, and so he began.

"Before you three little ones joined us, Land, Sea, Max and I happened to give an evil slave driver called Manslow his just rewards. But we did not know then that the slave driver had already sold young Land and Sea here to Ernest the Terrible, the most feared pirate and scoundrel on the ocean at that time. So we sailed '*Transom*' and delivered our cargoes, not knowing that we were being followed and he was slowly gaining on us. We finally met in the Straits of Hammerguard, and two more brave boys I have yet to meet. Land and Sea were at risk of being taken as slaves, but the four of us went to work on that crew. Actually, they were mostly all slaves themselves and they turned on their masters to fight with us. But Ernest the Terrible himself was trying to hide in a secret hatch when Land found him, and sent him sprawling with a good kick on his behind. Land hoofed him all around the deck, until Ernest was earnestly begging for mercy. His ship was taken over by her head slave, whom Ernest had treated abominably, and you all know the ship I mean. Her name is '*Wave Blazer*'."

La Chocolat and Roly gazed wide-eyed at each other. The Chocolate Ambassador had told them the story of how their Uncle Enrique, the Captain of '*Wave Blazer*', had been set free by the fearless crew of a merchant schooner, and now commanded the ship he had been captive on. But they had no idea that his rescuers were none other than their own dear Captain, Max and the Explorers!

"What ever happened to Ernetht the Terrible?" whispered Star.

"He joined Manslow in the Ghastly Prison of Bastille. Last I heard, all of the pirates were set to work building a new palace for the Prince of Perinia's wives."

They all laughed, but if you were still peeking through the porthole, you might have noticed that La Chocolat had drawn her little brother close, and that there were tears glistening on his cheeks.

Sea squeezed in next to them and wiped away Roly's tears with his hand. "We're going to miss you, you know," he said, and wrapped Roly in a great big hug.

Land leaned over and took the little boy's hand in his bigger rougher sailor's one. "Roly Poly, it does not matter how far you are away, you are always part of our crew. And we will look forward to holidays, and try to save all our adventures for when you are on board."

"Who's to say that Roly doesn't have adventures of his own at school?" threw in Captain Antonio.

Roly Poly brightened and looked up. The children dried their eyes and nodded. Then an indignant Star huffed, "Your adventureth had better not be ath exciting as ourth, becauth we can't share them with you ever!" Max barked two quick yips in agreement.

And so, '*Transom*'s' crew laughed loud and hugged each other tight, and bound together by all their adventures past—and those still to come—they gave heartfelt thanks for all they had and for the friends and family they loved more than their own lives.

Chapter 6
'*Transom*' to the Rescue!

On a clear late autumn's day, '*Transom*' prepared to sail a long trip across the Restless Ocean to deliver a cargo of ground potato flowers. The crew were downright sad getting ready for this particular voyage because Roly Poly had gone to school. Max was being no help at all, as the Great Dog had buried himself inside Roly's blanket, so that only his big tan rump and long tail showed hanging off the bunk. La Chocolat felt like joining him as she missed her little brother terribly, but she was carrying a new kind of truffle for delivery to the Ocean King's court and so was kept busy loading her boxes safely. As a result—once delivered—the new truffle became the Great Ocean King's favourite, and his signature chocolate for a long, long time. Even now, if you mention a certain cream and plum cocoa delight anywhere near the ocean, the Mer people will all stop what they are doing and swim towards you immediately.

But that all started after '*Transom*'s' Restless Ocean rescue, once La Chocolat had delivered them.

As the schooner slipped her moorings, the entire crew felt the absence of a certain happy smile. Once they were under way, Captain Antonio tooted a message on the foghorn, and so everyone tumbled into the cockpit.

"Crew, we are all a bunch of right drips! Roly needs to go to school, but he will be waiting for us when we dock at Tikkle-On-Sea. We all miss him terribly. But we still have each other, and I for one would not change that for the world."

The girls hugged him tight, and Land and Sea thumped him manfully on the back. With lifted spirits, they went about their work and were a bit more tender and a bit more understanding to each other than usual, glad to be reminded of what they should still be thankful for.

The days passed calmly and pleasantly. Then one day, Star noticed clouds on the horizon. She pointed them out carefully, as they were rather more like a little bit of steam from a kettle at that stage. But her eyes were shining and Captain Antonio knew that meant to listen well. More than once had Star's shining eyes saved them and so he ordered all hatches battened, goods stowed and lifelines for all, just in case.

'*Transom*' sailed on dependably and sure enough, mighty gusts of wind soon whipped salty spray high in the air. Land, Sea and Captain Antonio hauled in as much sail as they could, whilst dirty grey clouds washed over the sky so low and wild that they tore themselves on the tiptops of '*Transom*'s' masts.

The storm that followed was not half as bad as they expected, especially after their experience on their voyage to Bear de Sol. The crew knew what to do, all of which they were good at and so came through the rather rough storm very well. That is not to say that at some points the girls were not terrified, or the Explorers did not worry. But Captain Antonio and Max remained confident through the eye-blinding lightning, ear-shattering thunder and torrents of icy rain, while the schooner was thrown about the ocean's surface like your bath duck when you hop into a beautifully full bath. So the crew drew on courage and strength they did not know they had, until they realised that the storm was over.

As the skies cleared and the waves pitched and tossed less, Captain Antonio felt a tingle begin in his toes that made his heart beat and his fingers tap.

From his post at the chart table, Sea hollered for Captain Antonio. "Listen to this! I think someone is in distress," said Sea, handing the radio headphones to the Captain. After listening thoughtfully for a minute or so, he whipped the headphones off and checked the chart on the table.

"This is a message from the paddle steamer '*Southern Belle*'. She is in trouble. About… HERE!" he rapped the chart sharply. "Sea, take a sextant reading, and Land, alter course towards her, top speed and pronto!"

And before you would have time to open your fridge and choose something to nibble on, Captain Antonio and his crew had '*Transom*' heading directly into the floundering steamer's course.

After a short while, Star called down from the crow's nest that she had spotted '*Southern Belle*'.

"She lookth very nithe, Ca'tan," Star lisped when she was back on deck. "She ith very low in the water though." This second observation made the crew all stop and shudder. Sailors do not like to think of things like sinking ships, especially after a storm.

'*Transom*'s' sails were pulled low and they approached the leeward side of the waterlogged steamer. She was truly lovely. Her two tall white funnels sent puffs of smoke from her burners showing that she was still under way. That was a very good sign. La Chocolat held the wheel steady while the Captain threw lines to '*Southern Belle's*' crew. '*Transom*' looked like a toy next to the gracious '*Belle*'. Captain Antonio and Land swung on board the steamer to check on what help was needed while Sea made sure their moorings were fast.

The steamer's Captain shook their hands gratefully. "We sprung a leak in the storm. I think we might have hit a whale. My ship is taking on water in her port hull forward compartment and we cannot seem to pump fast enough. I was just wondering whether we should abandon ship, when your message came through. With the thought of one hundred passengers in lifeboats on this Restless Ocean, I was mighty relieved to hear from you."

Antonio and Land exchanged glances. If this well-known and worthy Captain Andy was at a loss, then there was not much chance that they could help. But they would certainly give the problem everything they had, as long as there was a ship and passengers to save.

"Let's go see the damage, shall we?" said Land. And so off they went.

Suddenly, '*Southern Belle*' shuddered and slowed. The smoke rising through the funnel from her port engine puffed and coughed, and got less and less. The water must have reached the burners. With no time to lose, the three sailors hurried to the holds below.

Water was pouring through what appeared to be a long and ominous crack in the majestic '*Belle's*' hull. All spare hands—some of them passengers—were pumping furiously. Land began measuring how long and how wide the crack was. Captain Antonio frowned thoughtfully, and then clicked his fingers as an idea popped into his head.

"I will be back in a moment," he said to Captain Andy. But that very troubled man hardly noticed. He was encouraging his men, issuing new orders, checking lifeboats and seemed to be everywhere at once.

Captain Antonio and Land hurried back on board '*Transom*' where he told his crew of his idea. In no time at all, they had rallied some able-bodied men from '*Southern Belle*' and were full steam ahead with putting the plan into action.

La Chocolat and Star opened the schooner's holds and directed helping hands while Sea organised a line of strong men from '*Transom*' all along to the '*Belle's*' port hold. Captain Antonio, meanwhile, went in search of Captain Andy to tell him of the plan and to prepare the rest of the crew with instructions.

Then, sacks of ground potato flowers were hauled up from '*Transom*'s' hold and passed quickly on from one man to the next, until the sacks found their way into the injured hull of the steamer. You see, potato flowers—if ground finely and kept dry—make the strongest glue that you could hope to find if mixed with salt and water.

For a long while, the men worked hard, some at the pumps, others passing sacks and still more shoring up the deadly crack. Eventually, just as each soul was beginning to give up hope that they would ever win this battle, the leak was slowed, and then finally stopped. Word was passed back down the line and through the ship, smiles brightened exhausted faces at the news and hope returned. Men pumped out water with renewed strength born from victory and soon a great cheer arose from aboard the steamer, as the last pump pumped out its last salty gallon back into the ocean where it should be. Then as if to say thank you, '*Southern Belle*' puffed and coughed, and smoke poured forth from both funnels as she gathered speed.

However, not all were heroes. There were some passengers aboard '*Southern Belle*' who complained and moaned loudly that their tea was cold, and that the steamer was too slow, and expected that all things should be as they pleased. But those will never know the true joy that better men feel, who bend their backs and use their hands when needed.

As Captain Antonio congratulated his crew on a job well done, nobody was more relieved—or more grateful—than Captain Andy. He held his hands over his heart, and was speechless. Star and La Chocolat took over from there, and in words never better said, gave him a big hug around his large middle and declared, "You are MOST welcome!"

Now there was the small problem of delivering only half of '*Transom*'s' cargo, but Captain Andy solved that one neatly. "The only potato flower buyer at Tikkle-On-Sea is my wife's second cousin by marriage and good farthings! – he can have the round the world voyage on board '*Southern Belle*' that he has been pestering me for since she was freshly launched. You can deliver my official invitation yourselves."

And so that was how Captain Andy's distant relative ordered a cargo that saved '*Southern Belle*'. After taking his distant relative on his round-the-world complimentary voyage, Captain Andy and his wife's second cousin by marriage launched another steamer and prospered beautifully together. The '*Belle*' kept on sailing—with her potato flower filled crack—until they were old and grey with wrinkles and walking sticks, and their sons and daughters took over the running of the business and prospered for generations after. But that evening, as '*Transom*'s' crew dined in five star style aboard the lovely steamer, they did not know that yet.

"Wait until Roly hears about this. He is going to be madder than a hornet to have missed saving this ship," laughed Sea.

They were all looking decidedly smart in their best clothes, even Max was in a top hat and bowtie, as they laughed together. They celebrated and were merry that night in the knowledge that the stars shone bright, the sky was clean, and that, today, they had made a difference.

Chapter 7
The Island of Glass

Mermaid Marguerite stood on '*Transom*'s' bow and attentively scanned the ocean ahead. The schooner should have been approaching the Great Glass Bubble that protected the Island of Glass.

'*Transom*' had been asked to help by the Mayor of the Island of Glass. A band of notorious sugar thieves had set their sights on the island, which made the Mayor and all of his subjects a little nervous. You see, the staple diet of Glassians is candy floss. Not the kind we know, however, theirs was spun from pure honey and frosted with fine cinnamon and nutmeg. The Mayor had met with Captain Antonio and his crew, who had talked with the Chocolate Ambassador, and together they had cooked up a cunning plan.

So here they were. Star and La Chocolat were threading large pieces of spiky coral onto lengths of rope while the Explorers were carefully checking suits of armour. Roly (who was on board for a while during his school holiday) and Max took turns trying on each helmet and giggling at each other before carefully taking them safely below decks. The Captain called up to Marguerite to see if she could spot the Bubble yet, to which she cried, "Yes, I think I do!"

Everybody sprang up and ran to the bows to catch a first glimpse of the Bubble. On the horizon, the sun was reflecting off something very large and as they drew closer, they could all see the majestic dome. The Island of Glass needed its dome for protection as everything on the Island was delicate, even the bees. The dome appeared to float on the waves and Captain Antonio steered '*Transom*' to the floating dock at its edge. You see, the only way INTO the Island of Glass, was to go UNDER the Bubble.

Once '*Transom*' was docked a small submarine surfaced next to her, and out popped a very official looking Glassian who said officially, "On the Mayor's service, I am here to escort you to him." With that they all piled on board and took their seats, strapped in, and as the submarine dived, they sat gazing wide-eyed at the under-ocean upon which they sail. Of course Marguerite could not ride with them, as she only had legs on board '*Transom*' and a long tail on a submarine might get in the way, so she dived off the schooner and followed them instead.

The children gasped in surprise at the glorious fish that surrounded them. As the ocean grew shallower on their journey, they could see a vibrant coral reef before them, and shafts of sunlight pierced the waters like spotlights in a carnival. Max barked at a dogfish, and they all exclaimed in delight as Mermaid Marguerite swam alongside and tapped the glass canopy. With a flip of her tail and a little wave, she pirouetted with a manta ray before swimming on.

When they arrived, their Glassian escort pointed them in the direction of a rather steep hill. Roly immediately ran off for a good romp in the clover fields with Max, Marguerite waved goodbye from the shore and off they went.

When they arrived on the hilltop, the Mayor and the Chocolate Ambassador stood together. "Everything is ready and in order, Captain. I hope the plan will work," said the Chocolate Ambassador. The Captain smiled and shook their hands firmly. "So do I," he said hopefully, and they all settled down to wait and watch.

From the tingling in his toes, our fearless Captain knew that they would not be waiting long.

Sure enough, Sea tapped him gently and pointed out far over the ocean to where they could just spot four tiny sails topping the horizon. The dome acted like a huge magnifying glass, alerting them to approaching danger rather quickly. The four sails were joined by three more, then eight more and another dozen, until the horizon was dotted with a fleet of plunderers, all heading their way. The men exchanged glances, nodded to each other and set off back down the hill. Marguerite was very soon joined by a noisy crew all boarding '*Transom*' and all talking at once in excitement.

"The sugar thieves are on their way," declared Captain Antonio by way of explanation.

Land stood by the helm and blew their emergency call on the foghorn, at which the crew all quietened and scurried inside to batten hatches and hide.

Soon they could hear the tumult of nasty, greedy thieves docking and then diving underneath the dome. After a while, the noise subsided. Captain Antonio nodded and Sea cautiously went to check that the thieves were inside the dome. Sea gave a dolphin whistle from the deck and everybody sprang into action, donning helmets and armour, and preparing to sail pronto. Marguerite kept a close eye out for any thieves. Twice the crew heard her break into clear and lovely song. Then, where thieves with muskets and arrows had been keeping watch, only tiny white feathers were left to blow about in the wind.

'*Transom*' sailed, and whilst Mermaid Marguerite steered her as close to the Bubble as she could; Antonio, Land and Sea took up the coral threaded rope and swung with all their might against the great dome while the girls shot arrows at the glass. At first, the coral and arrow heads just bounced off, but as they sailed on around its edge, the dome began to show tiny cracks. Soon arrows and coral were hitting the dome with resounding cracks. Slowly at first, and then faster and faster cracks began to deepen. Around the huge dome they sailed and worked, and the cracks snaked up the dome and got bigger.

Suddenly, they heard an earth-shattering CRACK! Mermaid Marguerite immediately steered '*Transom*' out to the open ocean and away from the dome, and in that moment great shards of falling Bubble began to throw up fountains of spray in the ocean around them. The crew were safe in their armour, and so they watched breathlessly, hoping that their plan was working.

Meanwhile, inside the dome the notorious sugar thieves were confused. They had been led to believe that this was a very large and wealthy island full of the sweetest of sugars and the finest of honeys, but they had arrived to nothing but an empty and deserted island. The army of mercenaries began to grumble. And just as they were standing on the hilltop scratching their heads, the dome high above began to crack. Great shards plummeted on top of the sugar thieves and their army. In panic, they ran backwards and forwards. They all tried to board the submarines but they swamped them and the submarines sank. Some dived into the water and swam to their ships to try and escape, but huge slivers from the dome cut through their ships, and they found themselves sinking.

There was no escape.

The last of the dome collapsed, and the notorious sugar thieves and their mercenaries were stranded on a little island with no means of escape. All of their ships were sunk in the Deep.

Mermaid Marguerite stood on '*Transom*'s' bow and attentively scanned the ocean ahead. The schooner should have been approaching the Great Glass Bubble that protected the Island of Glass. But this time, she was looking for the real one.

Once more, their Glassian submarine escort guided the crew to the Mayor. As they approached the Mayor's crystal palace, its fragile beauty held them all spellbound. Gasping in delighted awe as they entered, the children gazed up into endless atriums where birds fluttered and tropical palms waved fronds around crystal chandeliers and draped loops of fine patterned silk. They were led to an enormous ballroom where the Captain and his crew were treated to a wonderful banquet with delightfully short speeches.

"Well, well Captain. The plan actually worked. I cannot believe that the entire fleet of sugar thieves and mercenaries fell for your decoy," laughed the Chocolate Ambassador.

Antonio explained to the Mayor's wife, "La Chocolat came up with the idea to make a fake dome of transparent candy, and the thieves' sugar compasses led them directly into the trap. Thanks to the Chocolate Kingdom, the Glassians are not in captivity to those mercenaries tonight," said Antonio, and lifted his honeyed punch in a salute to the Chocolate Ambassador.

But what happened to the sugar thieves and mercenaries? With nothing to do all day except to play in the waves, and nothing to eat except great pieces of transparent candy, a curious thing happened. First one, then another and then a few more, and finally ALL of those grumpy sugar thieves found that they were HAPPY. They laughed and frolicked with dolphins and played together, and all thought of evil and bad was dispelled from their hearts forever. And so when they were rescued, they were henceforth known as The Band of Happy Sailors, and they all lived happy lives thereafter.

And so, through that long and joyous night, a certain crew danced away the hours. The Glassians celebrated their freedom, and as morning rays shone through a noble and strong dome, joy, peace and happiness remained.

Chapter 8
'Transom' on Holiday

Captain Antonio was being very secretive. Usually he discussed '*Transom*'s' cargo and destination with the whole crew so that they could all send letters, buy things like sun cream or shark repellent or an umbrella, depending on what they would need where they were going. But this time, the Captain was decidedly quiet on the subject of their next port. He even told the crew to stay strictly on board and went out with Max to do all the shopping for their next voyage himself. Very peculiar! If the Captain was not the Captain, and if he was any other person other than himself, the crew would all have been worried. However, all that they could really do was bounce with excitement, as this certainly meant he had a plan up his sleeve.

Land suggested sitting on Antonio and tickling him until he told all. Sea thought that making him a big cream cake and then not allowing him to eat any until he told all, would do the trick. But La Chocolat—the voice of reason as always—said, "I vote that we let him tell us when he is ready. If I know him at ALL, he is cooking up a nice surprise for us and to find out too early would spoil the fun for him."

The wisdom of her opinion could not be argued, and so to their chores with hearts singing they went.

Captain Antonio and Max arrived back with boxes and bags of every shape and description. They stowed them in the cargo hold, whistling and humming happily. Star peeked out of the hatch once and noticed a certain pair of feet with tapping toes, which meant that toes tingled which made her smile and giggle.

WHAT were those two up to?

"Right crew, what in thunder and lightning are you hiding down here for? Let's get some sails up and out into them waves!" bellowed Captain Antonio. His eyes sparkled with such glee and Max looked so smug that the crew were jumping around and loosing moorings, tying ropes, hauling sails and winding winches faster than you could pick a TV channel.

The schooner surfed through lazy waves, and if you have been on the ocean, you will know what I mean by a ship surfing through the waves; because once you have felt that feeling, you never forget it. It is as impossible to describe as what a bird thinks while flying but is sort of the same feeling as the best sleep you ever had in your life and that moment when you wake up and find yourself smiling—simply because you are happy and uncaring right then. So at that moment, without a cargo to check or readings to take, or weather to be concerned or not concerned about, Land, Sea, Star and La Chocolat simply swayed about in the cockpit with the rhythm of the ship. Soon they were lulled to sleep like dominoes, curled up together and dozing very contentedly. Captain Antonio at the wheel winked at Max, who grinned back in a wide doggy smile, and he checked his compass again.

After half a day's sail with the wind in the right direction, '*Transom*' should have sighted a rocky shoreline and so Captain Antonio kept a sharp eye. By now his drowsy crew had woken up, in the sort of hazy daze that always comes with relaxing. Land and La Chocolat rested their backs against the forward mast and talked nonsense lazily. Sea and Star were brewing some tea, and so were up shortly with mugs and rusks for all. Sea placed Max's rusk carefully on the end of his snout, and Max balanced the treat there for a moment before tossing the rusk into the sky and catching it neatly in his mouth. Star giggled delightedly and gave Sea half of her rusk, demanding, "Again, again! Pleathe?"

La Chocolat tossed her spiral curls out of her eyes and shook her head. "Men!" she huffed jokingly, and they all laughed.

Then Captain Antonio shouted, "Rocks ahoy!" and if the ship had been struck by lightning, the response would have been less entertaining. Land, Sea, La Chocolat and Star all leapt up and each ran for their emergency action stations. But then, the Captain was laughing, and so they looked around them and at once all caught their breaths.

They were sailing towards an island, more precisely a bay ringed by a band of creamy coloured sand. But the extraordinary thing was the colour of the ocean bay itself—the water shimmered in waves of turquoise, emerald and aquamarine—in some places the colour of sand and in others the grey of the very deep Deep. Inside the shelter of the bay, the water was as still as glass.

Star first noticed a grand yacht anchored a little way inside the bay. They were sailing towards her. "Ca'tan, who is that?" she asked.

"You will very soon see," he replied.

Antonio ordered the sails furled and the anchor dropped and when all was done, he lifted their signal flag and waved high.

On board the yacht came a replying flag waving in the air from what seemed to be a tiny, far away person. "Wait a minute… That's Roly Poly! And Mama and Papa!" yelled La Chocolat, leaping up and waving back. An infectious giggle carried across the water to them and then everyone was laughing and talking at once with excitement.

"Captain, you are a sneak! How did you organise this?" asked La Chocolat.

"Well, I felt that you kids all needed a good old-fashioned holiday. Marguerite found out about this place and knew that you would all love being here. If all we have heard is true, this island should be just fabulous. So we decided to keep everything a secret and wait until Roly was on holiday from school, so that your whole family could come."

The girls began jumping up and down like they had fleas in their brookies, shouting, "YAAAAYYYY!" at the top of their lungs, while Land and Sea were laughing out loud in sheer excitement. Captain Antonio summed it all up by doing a bomb dive overboard and wetting them all in his spray. Roly and the Chocolate Ambassador were next, and before long they were all splashing, dunking, diving and rolling in the tropical warmth of the blue, blue ocean. Then Mermaid Marguerite had joined them, and they played and played until they were all wrinkly.

Each day that followed, for a whole month afterwards, was packed with discovery, fun and adventure. When they explored the Island, they found in the midst of a coconut palm jungle a bubbling hot-spring surrounded by tall spikes of stone, and so they called this magical place the Island of The Needle Rocks.

They found beaches strewn with shells and rock pools filled with tiny fish of all colours. In the ocean, they dived on an underwater world of coral and rock caverns that were homes to octopii and eels, where frilly and plain fish of every size and colour darted about in frenzied swarms. When they walked on the sand, the grains jumped and tingled beneath their toes, and at night the waves glittered and shone with phosphorescence like the light of a million stars.

Night time was extra special, as they collected driftwood from the shore and made a bonfire with flames that flickered like the Northern Lights. Then they told stories, made up daft jokes, shared dreams and laughed over coffee and chocolates and a fine rum for the adults.

Captain Antonio and Mermaid Marguerite had thought of everything that the children could wish for. They had brought tents for camping in the deep green forest, and enough lollipops and bubble gum for them all to chew and crunch for a month of Sundays. They brought delicious treats and yummy things to snack on, lovely clothes for the girls to bathe in and fabulous trunks for the boys with pockets where they could keep all the treasures they found while swimming and exploring.

Then curled up in bunks after sun-drenched lazy days, they all slept the sleep of cradled babes.

The Island of the Needle Rocks was to be—in the memories of '*Transom*'s' crew—a truly special holiday.

From then on, each time the Captain asked the crew if they could guess where they were going, they all yelled at the top of their lusty lungs, in hopeful chorus, "Needle Rocks!"

One day, Captain Antonio promised himself, the answer would be, "YES!"

Chapter 9
How *'Transom'* is Stolen

A fine ocean breeze and gentle swells sent *'Transom'* into the Port of Guido. Each of the crew was eager to get to harbour for all different reasons. There was chocolate waiting, which meant La Chocolat would see her parents and Roly Poly. Land and Sea had recently fixed their old battered shotgun and wanted to try some hunting in the Guido forest. Max had been dreaming very many dreams of chasing rabbits in long grass and was longing to stretch his legs. And the Captain was waiting for word on a special new paint for his ship.

Only Star Princess was not happy to be going to Guido. She put her arms around Captain Antonio's neck while he sat at the wheel.

"Ca'tan, we should not go here. I don't feel good."

If Captain Antonio had been looking at Star, he would have seen that her eyes were shining with the brightness of constellations and if he had seen that, he would have listened, but he did not—and so began another adventure.

By the time *'Transom'* was moored, the crew were in agonies of excitement. They unloaded their cargo of Giggle Spice and began filling the hold with preserved Grasshopper Dandelions, bound for the Insect Sanctuary of Rangouse. This happened all too slowly for the crew and eventually, Captain Antonio and Star offered to stay on board while the others went ashore. Barely were the words out of the Captain's mouth than they were gone. They left in such a hurry that La Chocolat's tea cup hung in the air for a second, before crashing to the deck with a surprised thud.

The Captain and Star looked at each other and giggled, and then put their backs to their work.

After finishing the job, the two of them were tired and ready for a nap. Star went below decks to curl up in a bunk and the Captain nodded off at his wheel.

Not long after, the Captain dreamed that swells were rocking '*Transom*'. He dreamed that they were sailing without a crew, and so he woke with a start.

What a shock he got! There were two rough and mean sailors on '*Transom*'s' deck, and they were indeed surfing on the wide open ocean. When he tried to move, he realised that his arms and legs had been tied together. His first thought was for Star Princess and dread filled his heart.

"Hey, you lout, this is MY ship and how dare you tie me and take her from harbour!" he yelled at the closest thief, while the other one was checking the foresail.

The man turned and laughed ugly and loud. "Not so invincible without your crew, are you now? A ship belongs to whoever boards her," he jeered.

Now the Captain is a resourceful fellow, and the tingles in his toes and the plans up his sleeve got his mind to thinking. "We will put this no-good pirating band somewhere where they cannot do harm ever again," he said to himself and his ship. '*Banjo*' rocked in agreement behind him. He turned around and looked thoughtfully at his trusty liquorice lifeboat. Then he turned over to lie on his tummy and peered deep into the water churning behind '*Transom*'s' stern. Ugly Mouth spotted his intense gaze and came closer to see what he was looking at. As Ugly Mouth leaned further over the rail, the Captain lifted up his trussed legs and knocked the pirate hard on the rump, pushing him clean off the schooner.

"Yeah! One down!" said Captain Antonio, nudging a life ring overboard for the unfortunate pirate. If his hands were free, the Captain would have slapped his thigh but he decided he could save thigh-slapping for later.

The other mean looking fellow was coming back. He looked around for Ugly Mouth and then looked menacingly at the Captain. "Where is he?" he demanded.

"He went below," replied the clever Captain. And so the other pirating thief charged off down the hatch muttering,

"That's what you get for putting a fool in charge of watching the prisoner."

With no time to rethink his plan, Captain Antonio rose awkwardly to his feet. This is no easy task on a rolling ship when your legs are tied together, you must know. Using both of his tied hands, he pulled himself up into the lifeboat and in the safety of '*Banjo's*' rocking hull, he began to work at untying the knots with his teeth.

"Thank heavens these fellows are not very clever," he thought, but he found his task hard to concentrate on while he grew more and more anxious about Star. Shortly, he was untied and free. He peeped over '*Banjo's*' edge and saw three pirating thieves scratching their heads and staring at the empty spot where he had been. Lying quietly on his back to think, he saw above him the rope that Land had tied for the children to hold on to when they went for swims in the ocean. Carefully, the Captain reached up and tugged the free end. He checked again on the pirates. They were searching the decks thoroughly, so he quickly slipped out of '*Banjo*', pulling the end of the rope with him and bolted for the hatch.

The pirates gave a cry and ran to catch him. As they closed in, he jumped in the air and swung on the rope in a wide swinging swoop. He kicked hard with his feet square on one scoundrel's chest and sent that no-good pirate reeling overboard. He cannon balled into another. This pirate was thrown back against the mast, knocking his head with a stout thud and crumpled to the deck with a silly grin all over his face. As the rope swung back, he dropped into the cockpit and scrambled down the hatch with the third pirate hot in pursuit. He slammed the hatch closed behind him and bolted the lock firmly in place. Now '*Transom*' has a particularly sturdy hatch, and so Captain Antonio knew that the pirates would take a while to work out a way to get through the thick oaken timbers.

Inside, the Captain turned to the cabin, expecting to find more scallywags to contend with. However, the saloon and galley were deserted. He did not call for Star, just in case she had managed to hide or escape, and so he crept through to the cabins. As he peeked into the passageway, he saw two more pirates running towards the forward hatch. They pulled themselves through and up onto the deck.

Captain Antonio then called, "Star Princess, where are you little one?" But there was no answer.

He called again, going to each of the cabins desperately and when he got to Mermaid Marguerite's cabin, he heard a muffled voice, "Ca'tan? Is that you?"

The little Princess had climbed onto Mermaid Marguerite's bunk to rest but was woken up—her eyes shining like fiery stars—just as the pirates had boarded '*Transom*'. With no time to warn anyone, the clever little girl had locked herself away inside the mermaid's locker, so that no pirate could see the light of her eyes and take her prisoner.

A very relieved Captain opened the tiny cupboard and snuggled her close. "I was so worried. We are not safe yet, but as long as you are okay we can button this up real quick."

So saying, he told her to stay hidden and safe, with instructions that when she heard their foghorn signal she could come out.

The pirates, however, had escaped in '*Banjo*'. They had locked up the hatches tight from the outside. Glancing out of the porthole, Antonio saw that '*Transom*' was fixed on a course for a deadly coral reef close by. But this was not the Captain's ship for nothing, and in the time that you would take to turn off your bedside light at night, he had slipped through his secret escape hatch and was pulling down sails almost as fast as the speed of light.

Running back to the wheel, he untied the thick rope holding the ship on her dangerous course and brought the graceful schooner hard around to port. Then he tooted for Star to join him. A jagged piece of coral scraped harmlessly at '*Transom*'s' side and Captain Antonio breathed a relieved sigh at their very narrow escape. Star was already hard at work on the winches, helping to reset the sails.

"Right, we have unfinished business young lady. No one gets left behind and that includes '*Banjo*'," stated the Captain to his tiny crew. "Go and fetch me my shotgun."

"But Ca'tan, your gun doethn't work," lisped Star. "Land couldn't fix the broken bit yet."

Eyes twinkling beneath his hat, Captain Antonio smiled. "Yes, but they don't know that."

And so Star Princess and Captain Antonio rescued '*Banjo*' and set those pirates floating on the unlikely life raft of left-over chocolate boxes instead. As they raised a sail, the Captain shouted to them that he would send a rescue boat from the Harbour Police once they got back.

'*Transom*' returned to harbour safe, and to a terribly upset crew. They already had Coast Guard and Police boats looking for the schooner. Roly had the Ocean Kingdom searching, and so they were all faint with relief when Sea spotted her mast on the horizon heading back to the port.

As for those good for nothing thieving pirates, they had been striking terror into the hearts of sailors and landlubbers alike and were the scourge of the ocean surrounding the busy port of Guido. A sizeable reward had been placed on their heads by the Mayor of Guido, so that their trade routes could get back to normal again.

With the reward, Captain Antonio repainted '*Transom*'s' hull with the special paint that the Chocolate Ambassador bought him. The colour of rich toffee, the special paint spread chocolate essence through the water to let Mer people know that the Chocolate Ship was nearby.

When the Coast Guard found the pirates afloat on a flotilla of chocolate boxes, they were being circled by a hundred different fish who were all making sure that they never bothered '*Transom*' ever again. The pirates all joined Manslow, the evil slave driver, in the deepest darkest dungeon of Bastille and have not been heard of since.

Chapter 10
The Ocean of Illusion

'*Transom*' and '*Wave Blazer*' were on their way to the Island of SingSong in the Ocean of Illusion with a full cargo of delicious food. Captain Antonio was the only captain on the ocean who could find the Island with no trouble. His very clever navigation, helped by the resident dolphins, kept the schooner on course and made '*Transom*' the only ship that the Mayor of the Island could rely on to deliver fresh fruit and pastries for their children without getting lost. '*Wave Blazer*' helped Captain Antonio with cargoes that were too large for '*Transom*'. Her captain was brave and loyal Enrique, the Chocolate Ambassador's brother.

And so, as naughty waves and a mischievous wind drove '*Transom*' on, two little faces peeked out of the forward hatch. Roly Poly and Star Princess glanced at each other, climbed out of the hatch and raced to the cockpit where the Captain and Max were checking ocean charts. There, the two children sat down quietly.

Not long afterwards, a very loud shriek of surprise followed by a yell of pain broke the peaceful morning. Roly and Star collapsed in helpless giggles, holding their tummies as if their laughter might split their sides. Captain Antonio lowered the chart he was holding and peering over the top of it said, "What on earth…? I think Land is in trouble down there. Off you go and take a look if he is okay."

Roly Poly hopped off his cockpit perch still giggling, but as he was about to reach the hatch, a very angry Land stormed into the cockpit from below deck. Roly and Star could not help themselves. They laughed so hard that even the Captain found difficulty not joining in.

Land was very wet and he sported a great red lump on his forehead. He glowered down at the two little ones. "So you are OBVIOUSLY responsible for this mischief, I see. I do not enjoy being attacked by a bucket of cold water when I wake up after a long night's watch! Another trick like that and I will smack your bottoms good and proper!"

At Land's outrage, the Captain could no longer contain himself. He let out a squeak and then a cough, and finally he let loose in belly shaking laughs. Max offered Land a paw in sympathy and licked the bump on his head affectionately. Only the Great Dog knew how upset he was.

Not long after that more mischief was brewing, however...

La Chocolat carried a platter of sliced fruit for breakfast but as she stepped out of the galley, she found herself sprawled on the saloon floor. Granadilla pips ran down her face and a banana was squashed on her cheek. Spoiled pieces of melon, grapefruit and strawberries rained down on her. As she picked herself up, Roly and Star's shouts of laughter echoed through the schooner.

Max bounded down the stairs and after licking the poor girl's face clean, he turned to the two mischievous children with a doggy harrumph. La Chocolat sat up and rubbed her ankles where she had tripped over a short piece of rope held by Roly and Star across the doorway. Max grabbed the rope in his teeth, bounded through the hatch and tossed the offending piece overboard with a growl.

But the fun was not over...

Sea sat on deck untangling a crow's nest of fishing line from catching their mackerel dinner the day before. He stretched as the kinks in his neck straightened out and then went below to get a new reel. As he stepped into his cabin, his bare feet squashed and squelched into some terrible goo. His feet slid from under him, flew into the air and he landed flat smack on his back. A chorus of laughter accompanied his misfortune, as he lay dazed wondering what had hit him. He was covered from head to foot in flour and water glue. Max was by Sea's side in an instant, whining his concern. Max nuzzled Sea with his nose and then let out a huge sneeze. Soon Max was sneezing and sneezing, with wheat flour rising in white clouds all around them.

Breakfast was late and La Chocolat was miserable. Land was out of sorts, Sea was still dazed and Max was covered in a sprinkle of flour that every now and then, he would stop and try to rub off of his nose after volleys of huge wet sneezes.

The Captain decided that the time had come for him to step in.

He folded up his charts, stashed them away and went in search of the two naughty children.

Roly was on the bow listening to directions from the dolphins. "Captain, we need to go that way," he said, his little nose crinkled and his eyes twinkling mischievously as he pointed off to port.

Captain Antonio forgot his errand and frowned. "Are you sure? I was certain we were on the right course but the Ocean of Illusion is a tricky one." And so saying, he hurried back to the helm to alter their direction to the one Roly showed him.

Roly lay on his tummy on deck, giggling with his fishy friends who leapt and rolled alongside the schooner. Star joined him and they lay side by side, whispering and cooking up more mischief.

After some time, Captain Antonio checked his position using his sextant. Frowning, he bellowed, "We are way off course. Roly, are you absolutely sure that the dolphins told you to alter direction?"

Well, the response the Captain got was not the one he wanted. Roly and Star laughed so much they snorted a little. They did not happen to notice that Captain Antonio's face was getting redder and his frown deeper until he exploded, "Off to the cabin with you both where you cannot work anymore of your mischief! You can come out on the next watch."

Land, Sea and the Captain quickly corrected their course after signalling '*Wave Blazer*'. Both ships raised extra sail to increase their speed. Land worked the winches while Sea stood at the wheel to bring '*Transom*' round to their new heading. The Captain was buried in charts, compasses and all sorts of important-looking instruments while he re-checked their correct course and worked out how else they could make up for their lost time.

Meanwhile, La Chocolat and Max were thinking and planning together in the galley. They made their way up to the cockpit, and when '*Transom*' and '*Wave Blazer*' were again safely heading towards SingSong Island, La Chocolat presented her plan to Captain Antonio, Land and Sea. With heads together, they whispered and giggled, and plotted and schemed, and with smiling faces they went on their ways about the ship.

When the watch changed, the Captain rang the ship's bell three times.

Land, Sea and La Chocolat quickly made their way to '*Transom*'s' stern and climbed into '*Banjo*'. Max loped into the cockpit and Captain Antonio helped the Great Dog into his position before joining the others in the liquorice lifeboat.

Roly and Star, who had been thinking upon their sins quietly in their cabins for what felt like a very, very, VERY long time, heaved sighs of relief and prepared to go back up on deck.

What a surprise waited for them!

As Max spotted them scampering up the steps of the hatch, he began a mournful howl that sent shivers down the spines of the entire crew. Max's front paws held the ship's wheel on course and his tail was tucked tightly underneath him. His big head was thrown back as he gave himself over to terrible sorrow.

If Max was an actor, he would have won an Oscar for his performance there and then. Roly and Star hurried to him, stroking his ears and laying their cheeks on his shoulders. "What ith WRONG Makth?" lisped Star in anguish. Then looking around, she added in surprise, "And where ith everybody?"

At this, Max howled louder and longer, and even more sadly. The two children stared wide-eyed at each other. Where was the Captain? Where were Land and Sea? Why was La Chocolat not busy in the galley? Roly began to run around the deck, calling out for the missing crew. Star sat in a heap next to Max and began to cry.

Inside '*Banjo*', the crew were writhing in laughter. "La Chocolat, this is the best payback ever," whispered Sea. "But I think we had better hop out before those two little ones get too frightened."

Captain Antonio nodded, and so on Land's count of three, they all shot their heads up over '*Banjo's*' hull and yelled, "SURPRISE!"

Star leapt up in fright. Roly tripped over a rope and nearly toppled overboard, but Max caught his shorts in his big laughing mouth. The crew fell out of the lifeboat in helpless giggles, but Star abandoned herself to floods of tears, and Roly frowned his most cross frown with his hands on his round hips and stamped one foot angrily.

Captain Antonio drew them both onto his lap. "Little ones, do you see that you may find playing jokes on others very funny, but are you happy when the joke is played on you?"

They both looked up at him guiltily, and shook their heads gravely. "We are very very thorry Ca'tan. We promith we will never hurt you again," lisped Star, and Roly wrapped his chubby arms around the Captain's middle and squeezed as hard as he possibly could.

And so, '*Transom*' and '*Wave Blazer*' arrived in SingSong Harbour just in time that the fruit was still fresh and the pastries still fragrant. That night for dinner, Roly and Star surprised the crew with an island delicacy, coral nectar champagne and sugar flowers for dessert.

"Well, I guess all that mischief in this mischievous ocean really paid off," said Land, raising his champagne glass. With that, Max slunk over and stole Land's last sugar flower clean off his plate. Everybody dissolved into laughter at Land's indignant, "HEY, Max! You skellem!"

A happy content crew climbed into their bunks that night. Good laughs, good food and good friends all added to the bubbly feeling that all was once again well on board.

Chapter 11
The End of the World

A certain very rich merchant from Tweentown Biffalloon sent word to '*Transom*' that he requested their services, and so the ship found herself docked in the strange little harbour. The harbour was hidden somewhere between the Equator and the clouds but far enough from each to be a part of neither. Captain Antonio had followed his charts very carefully indeed, and so here they were.

The rich merchant wasted no time. He offered them all the gold of his sizeable fortune, if they could find his son. As the merchant and the Captain walked through the town's market, they spoke quietly.

"The lad was last seen on board my flagship, '*Aquila Spice*', some time ago. The ship was rumoured to have been fallen upon by pirates and scuttled. '*Aquila Spice*' was en route to New Wood carrying fine fabric, but she and her crew were never heard of again. Not a day goes by when my wife and I do not pray for our boy, and I must believe he lives. He is a strong and noble lad, and our only son. But his loyalties lie openly with the True Emperor, so I fear that Master Yeken may have caught up with him."

Here the merchant and Antonio exchanged knowing glances. Not many would brave crossing Yeken, and so Captain Antonio now understood why the rich merchant had taken the time to seek him out in particular, for this very dangerous mission.

As '*Transom*' again set out for adventure—this time in the trail of '*Aquila Spice*'—Captain Antonio and Land discussed their mission and studied their maps while Sea cleaned their guns and sharpened their knives. The Captain told the crew all he could about their mission and from the tingling in his toes, he assured them that adventure was not far away. Star was sent up to the crow's nest to keep a sharp eye for, well, anything out of the ordinary.

Star noticed a thick mist on the horizon. At first, she thought that the mist was a storm, but as they drew nearer she alerted Land. "That is no normal fog," said Land, "Best we prepare. Captain Antonio says no charts exist for the ocean beyond."

The crew all assembled on deck. With '*Transom*'s' sails pulled low, they held their breaths and only with faith in their good Captain—whose toes tingled mightily and who did not flinch on their approach—did they enter the legendary mist at the End of the World.

'*Transom*' ploughed dependably into the fog.

Roly suddenly shouted from the bowsprit. They hurried forward and what a sight lay before them! The ocean fell away beneath and it seemed that '*Transom*' should plummet to a splintery end. The mist was formed by a spray that only a vast ocean of water falling to endless depths can make, and yet all was silent and still. La Chocolat hugged her little brother in fright, the Explorers held their breaths, Star hugged Max and the Captain closed his eyes in dread.

But instead of plummeting over the edge, '*Transom*' glided on.

Several moments passed in silence before the crew realised that the air was still and they had come to a complete stop, suspended in nothingness. Silence cloaked the ship and when La Chocolat spoke, the mist seemed to absorb her voice so that her words sounded like a muffled whisper.

"I think we should try to row. Pirates that I was once captured by told a tale of how you row through the mist at the End of the World."

So they did. Through this strange silent suspension, they rowed for three days and when they slept, '*Transom*' stopped, quietly waiting.

On the third day, Star lisp-shouted from the bow, "Ca'tan, I can thee light!"

Land and Sea were quite exhausted from a long spell rowing, so they took a rest against their oars. Then sure enough, a dull yellow light broke through and shone eerily onto them. The schooner seemed to shudder and as she glided out from the mist, they were suddenly enveloped in noise, as though they had opened a door and sound rushed in. Shouting, clanging, banging, squeaking of machines, clanking of chains and the hissing of steam greeted them. '*Transom*' glided right up to a suspended dock around which were moored many vessels of all different kinds, chained and locked to the dock. Just next to them rested a magnificent tall ship, her lovely appointment and graceful lines defying the chains that seemed to hold her captive. She was a ship built for speed and cargo, a merchant's dream.

Toes tingling mightily, the Captain stepped onto the mysteriously suspended jetty. Towards him swaggered three louts, and they were definitely not intending to be friendly. Land took the girls and Roly to the cabins for safety and told them to stay hidden, whatever happened.

He returned on deck just in time to see Captain Antonio being hustled away at gunpoint by a nasty-looking lout. Land's hands angrily balled into fists, but Sea put an arm across Land's chest to stop him and pointed to two more nasty looking fellows left behind to guard '*Transom*'. So the Explorers stood by and waited until Antonio was taken down the jetty ladder and out of sight.

And then, of course, in no time at all their two guards were mowed down like dandelions in a hurricane. In the shake of a lamb's tail, Land, Sea and Max had them trussed like Christmas turkeys and locked into the suspended jetty's tiny guard room. The Explorers armed themselves with weapons, and with Max, Roly and the girls staying on board to guard their ship, Land and Sea leapt off into a world of adventure.

As they climbed down the suspended jetty, they stood spellbound at the sight that lay far, far below them.

On the horizon, there stood a majestic castle surrounded by the walls of a city. From all the activity below them, the Explorers came to the conclusion that the city and the castle were being built by the many slaves that toiled beneath loads and pulled wagons of rock-hewn bricks.

Quickly the two lads hurried down the ladder, taking care to stay well hidden from any they thought could be guards. Then they disguised themselves in the strange clothes of this new place, smeared mud on each other and each took up a heavy load. The Explorers were then free to wander unnoticed by the guards among the hard-working slaves. They whispered questions here and there to the slaves, until they understood all that they needed to. Then the two fearless lads stole behind a deserted shed and laid their plan.

The evil Master Yeken had sent his mercenaries throughout the earth, looking for a strong workforce to build his castle and a vast city at the End of the World. Once through the mist, there was only one way out, across a bridge that could not be found unless one had a south-facing compass carved of whalebone. All those who stood for Goodness and Truth were captured and brought to this place as Master Yeken's slaves. They were gathered from far and wide, but Land and Sea learned that one man knew of the way to freedom. That one was kept prisoner locked in a solitary cell under constant guard. The Explorers also learnt where all new arrivals were taken.

And sure enough, Captain Antonio was being led to a grim and stinking gaol quite near the castle. He was given some rough treatment actually, and the lout was good at saying very nasty things indeed. But there was some mighty tingling going on you-know-where, and so he patiently endured all the discomfort and abuse. Lout told him that he and his crew were now slaves to the Grand Master Yeken and that they would be staying at the End of the World until the Master's city was built—which really meant forever. With a raucous laugh, he threw the Captain into a dark cell with four other men and set off to fetch the rest of '*Transom*'s' crew.

However, Captain Antonio is not one to stop and lick his wounds, and so he went to work right away at finding a means of escape. In not very long, he found that the prison door was bolted into the stonework of the walls, and that those bolts needed a fair effort to loosen them, but loosened they could be. Enlisting the help of his fellow prisoners, together they took stock of what tools they could muster. With a rusty spoon, a coin and a piece of bone from a long-ago forgotten dinner, they fell to working the bolts out of the wall. Eventually, they all steadied themselves with good grips on the iron bars and heaved the door out with an almighty bang.

As they hurried out, a voice yelled to Antonio from beneath a grate set deep into the floor. "Please take me with you! I know the way back, I can help you!" Captain Antonio looked around for help from the other prisoners with him, but they were wrestling three guards to the ground further along the grimy passage.

The Captain wasted no time. He snatched a large ring of keys from a hook on the wall and began to fit them to the lock in turn, until he found the right one. The two soon found themselves stealing out through the gaol, stopping to unlock all the doors along the way to free the prisoners inside.

While the Captain was busy freeing prisoners, and locking up the guards instead, the Explorers made their way through the city, quietly spreading word of their plan to the slaves.

When word was widely and well spread, they made their way back to '*Transom*'.

***

Throughout Yeken's city, something was happening. As the whispers spread, slaves began to pick up their feet and eyes brightened.

Hope had finally come to the End of the World.

Chapter 12
The Fall of Yeken

The Explorers reached '*Transom*' but the schooner was deserted. Had the children been taken captive?

"Not on Max's watch, if I know him at all. MAX!" yelled Sea. Immediately, they spotted a great head emerge with a 'Woof!' from above the railing of the tall ship. Max had taken the children to the tall ship, and they were all busy undoing her chains. Land and Sea hurried over to help and explained their plan.

When they were done and the tall ship was free, Land took up the foghorn. The brothers paused for a moment and looked at one another. Then Sea nodded.

"Let it rip!" he exclaimed, and with a deep lungful of air, Land blew as hard as he could for as long as he could, and '*Transom*'s' emergency signal reverberated again and again throughout the End of the World.

As Antonio, the stranger and a hoard of freed prisoners emerged from the gaol, they heard the foghorn blowing. A slave close by yelled, "The Signal! To arms, one and all!" and with that slaves turned on the guards, felling them with gusto and dragging them to the gaol.

The Captain smiled and slapped his thigh. "Clever boys. To the ships, double quick!"

The stranger yelled as they ran, "Follow me, I know the way!"

With throngs of men, they arrived to find Land on '*Transom*' and Sea on the tall ship with oars prepared. As many hands as they could fit jumped on board, while others cut chains with Sea's axe and manned other ships along the dock. The stranger caught sight of '*Transom*' and went as pale as a sheet. But he did not hesitate. He leapt on board the tall ship and took charge, directing the oarsmen towards the mist. The stranger then opened a tiny compartment well-hidden at the end of one of the ship's huge booms, and reaching in, he retrieved an unusual looking compass—carved of whalebone and pointing South—and a chart. Consulting these carefully and after several course changes, he directed the ship's oarsmen to stop. Then he waved on all the ships behind him to go ahead on into the mist.

"The Bridge is here! Row on through the mist!" he bellowed.

Captain Antonio on '*Transom*' came to a stop next to the tall ship, both decks crowded with more men than they thought the ships could ever hold. Below them the city was emptying fast.

Land and Sea had spread the word that at the foghorn signal, the enslaved men were to capture their guards, lock them in the gaol, release the prisoners held there and then hurry to the docks where they could board ships to escape. They were sure that the Captain, once free, would hurry back to the ship. They could then find the one who knew the way out of the End of the World, and together form an army to fight their way out if needed. Then they could escape with the freed slaves and hopefully gain news of the merchant's son.

Shiploads of free men glided past them, shouting their thanks and farewells while the stranger and the '*Transom*' crew kept watch for any sign of attack by Yeken's men. When they were sure that every last freed slave had sailed safely through the bridge, the stranger motioned '*Transom*' forward. As the mist closed over the schooner, Captain Antonio looked back towards the castle. Standing on the top turret was Yeken himself. His red cape billowed around him as he returned the Captain's steady gaze, one hand holding a long throwing spear. Captain Antonio raised his hand in a long and final salute to the man who had once - long ago - intended him grave harm. But then '*Transom*' was shrouded in mist herself, and the stranger followed closely behind. As the tall ship rowed over the bridge, the stranger stood on the stern and threw handfuls of blue ocean rock as far as he could. As the rock hit the bridge, it smouldered and great chunks of bridge broke off and floated up around them and through the mist. Then quite suddenly, the mist began to rain. The stranger bellowed for them all to raise sail and row as fast as they could, as the mist would not hold them for much longer. Then they found themselves rocked and sprayed by their very own waves again. As the mist fell to the ocean, all who could gazed in awe as they watched the destruction of the city and of Yeken, right hand man to the Evil Emperor.

Like a house of cards, years of back-breaking toil were mowed down to nothingness, as waves washed over that place of evil desolation and rid the earth of it. Then the men were sailing on swiftly, and attentions were back on things more important, and they left the Great Ocean to sweep in and claim back her own bed…

And the End of the World ceased to exist as surely as the memories of a bad dream go with the light of day.

'*Transom*'s' crew swung across to their own ship, as '*Transom*' and the tall ship drew abreast of each other. Captain Antonio shouted an invitation to the stranger to join them for a meal, hoping for word on the merchant's son. And so over smoked salmon steaks and new potatoes washed down with Star's finest ale, there unfolded a story of courage and bravery that showed a noble heart.

For the stranger was himself the rich merchant's son, Jacques, and the tall ship was none other than '*Aquila Spice*'.

A long while before, Jacques had learnt of the slavery at the End of the World and had sought all the knowledge he could of Yeken's kingdom. He found that blue ocean rock was the only way to destroy the bridge from their world and had set out to free the captives with bags of blue ocean rock and many weapons hidden in the hold amongst his cargo of beautiful fabrics. The compass and chart he had searched for diligently, and with the help of Pip and the AOE (Aerial Organisation for Earth), had found them. Jacques learned of their existence from a former mercenary who was now a Happy Sailor, thanks to a diet of candy on a certain deserted island. The Happy Sailor was very helpful to Jacques in planning this heroic rescue mission.

But Yeken had spies everywhere and had heard of Jacque's intent, and before they found the mist, '*Aquila Spice*' was fallen upon by Yeken's mercenaries. All of Jacque's men were taken hostage and held in the gaol. His plan was defeated before he had begun. And yet here he sat—FREE.

"Captain Antonio," finished Jacques, smiling widely, "I do believe my instructions to you were to keep yourself and this very valuable ship safe. But '*Transom*' looks just fine to me, and you have my deepest gratitude. And what's more, you have earned yourself '*Aquila Spice*' as your prize. However, I would be much happier if you don't try a stunt like that again, at least not on board '*Transom*'."

The schooner's crew realised that this was the very man who had sent '*Transom*' to the Captain many, many moons ago, and their mouths dropped open in disbelief. The Captain himself shook Jacques' hand strongly, and the two men fell to talking all manner of nautical nonsense and became the fastest of friends on their voyage back to Tweentown Biffaloon. And the courage of Captain Antonio and his crew earned them more gold than both '*Transom*' and '*Aquila Spice*' could hold—true to the rich merchant's word when he welcomed his son home.

But that was later. Throughout that first starlit night of freedom, joyful eel mails were despatched around the world post-haste to parents, wives, children and sweethearts, from men thought lost forever, while on board '*Transom*' the crew sat with their guest as they ate, drank and were merry.

Chapter 13
The Captain's Birthday

'*Transom*' rocked gently with a creamy spray tickling her bow as she ploughed through a peaceful ocean. She was just outside the Port of Knod, where an eternally sleepy village awaited her cargo of winter bed bonnets. Captain Antonio leaned over his ship's bowsprit and tried to catch salty spray in his cupped hand. Max held his huge head up to the wind and barked excitedly with the anticipation of a good gallop soon.

The schooner's crew were all fully occupied with scrubbing the ship, spick and span ready for mooring. Only La Chocolat noticed the Captain sitting on the bow. This was very unlike him to be dreaming, just before they entered harbour. Usually, his good-humoured orders issued from the wheel added to the excitement of new ports. But today, on his birthday, Captain Antonio felt old and very tired.

After destroying the End of the World and Master Yeken along with it, '*Transom*'s' crew held the hope that the evil in the world would somehow abate, and Goodness and Truth would prevail. But this was not to be. Since the loss of Master Yeken, the Evil Emperor seemed more intent than ever to hunt down Captain Antonio and fail not in the trying. The past voyages had been fraught with close encounters by pirates, thugs and informers. It took all the Captain's energy and quick thinking to keep ship and crew safe and stay one step ahead of those intending to do them harm.

And frankly, he was wondering if he was up to the task of protecting them all.

La Chocolat took the Captain a steaming mug of hot chocolate and two truffles, one for him and one for Max, as the Great Dog always gave her a mournful look of decidedly hurt feelings if he did not get one.

"A penny for your thoughts?" she joked as she approached the bowsprit.

The Captain gave a start of surprise and sat up to take the mug, his hazel eyes troubled. "Well well, I thought you would be in your cabin knitting doilies for your hair and putting on smellies with Star. I was just thinking, how lucky I am that I have you lot." La Chocolat wrapped her arms around his shoulders, and Max put his big paw on the Captain's knee. The three smiled at each other and Antonio ruffed Max's neck.

But as La Chocolat took the empty mug back to the galley, she knew that their brave Captain needed to let his hair down and have some fun. She smiled smugly, and passing Land and Sea working on deck, she nodded and gave them a thumbs up. They grinned back, eyes flashing mischievously with their secret.

The graceful schooner glided to her mooring in the tiny picturesque town, and everyone went about their work cheerfully with an edge of anticipation and excitement hurrying them along nicely. Land despatched Captain Antonio to the Mayor, saying, "Captain, Max is nearly beside himself to go ashore. Why don't you head on up to see the Mayor about our cargo and I will sort out all the off-loading here."

"Good idea. I reckon I will!" said our intrepid Captain, secretly itching to explore through the tight twisty-turny lanes and ancient stone houses in the famous village of Knod. With a slap on his thigh and a tip of his hat, he whistled for Max and the two were off faster than you would start out on an Easter Egg hunt.

And then the crew really did get to work.

As evening closed in, *'Transom'* found herself blanketed in darkness after all the frantic activity of the afternoon. Lazy ripples licked the ship's hull and peace filled the harbour, as yawning Knoddians were tucked into bed. The harbour had filled up surprisingly during the afternoon with all manner of interesting people, and the crew waited anxiously for the Captain's return.

You see, on board the schooner right then were shiploads of the best people, the salt-of-the-Earth people that everybody wishes they really had as true friends, but seldom ever do.

When all was ready, Sea reached for the foghorn and blew their emergency signal loud and clear. Of course '*Transom*'s' crew knew that the Captain's toes would have been tingling mightily all day, and that he had been expecting an adventure to jump out and beg him to follow. And they knew that he would hurry as fast as he could back to the ship when he heard the call.

Sure enough they did not have long to wait. In a hop and a skip from a grasshopper, they heard Max's bark and a laugh from Antonio echo down the streets to the quiet and still port.

La Chocolat made sure everyone was ready. Star had to close her eyes as they were shining so brightly that she lit the ship up all by herself. Roly giggled and giggled like a happy river.

As Antonio strode around the corner of a particularly interesting ancient stone house and into the harbour, the air exploded with light and music and colour! Even the Knoddians stopped snoring in their beds—just for a second, mind – but they talk of the interruption to this day.

You see, Land was holding a great handful of strings which he tugged at the instant he spotted Captain Antonio. Immediately, two entire ships began to transform into a fairyland of tiny yellow lights: little glass jars were strung in neat rows and suspended high overhead, and filled with hundreds and hundreds of sleepy fireflies. At Land's tug, they all began to wake up and glow. From '*Transom*'s' bow to her stern, and around her masts to their tips, and draped down in a fairy-light tent, over her decks and into the water, hung streamers of glowing tiny firefly-lights. Moored next to '*Transom*', also lit up like a magical Christmas tree, rested the Captain's tall ship '*Aquila Spice*'. She had slipped into harbour for the event during the afternoon.

Sea held a fuse and a match, which he lit at the same time that Land woke up the fireflies. With a satisfying bang, fireworks launched high in the air, exploded in huge fountains and lit up the sky. Red, green, yellow, orange and blue were reflected in the still harbour, and then suddenly the reflections became ripples and splashes...

And then, ocean creatures of every size and shape were leaping out of the water and did somersaults and corkscrews, squeaking and honking, and snorting and bleating at the top of their aquatic voices. There were whales blowing fine mist spouts and sailfish doing acrobatics. Marlin opened their majestic fins that shone, while tiny sardines frolicked on the surface with their poetic whistles giving the whole atmosphere a joyful light-heartedness.

Then Star opened her eyes.

The air immediately fizzed into sparkles darting every which way, and the sparkles found Captain Antonio who stood with his mouth wide open in surprise, and Max who was jumping in the harbour shallows and had his muzzle deep in the water trying to catch the firework reflections. As the sparkles led the two gently to the ship, a hundred strong voices joined to sing, "Happy birthday, happy birthday to the best and wisest Captain on the wide and open Ocean Deep!"

In a backdrop of shooting stars, there commenced a celebration for life and hope that has never been seen before or since.

La Chocolat filled champagne glasses and everyone became solemn, as Captain Antonio boarded his schooner.

Mermaid Marguerite stepped forward, and the brave and intrepid Captain caught his breath...

She wore her official crown, and from the top of her lovely head to the tip of her diamond-shod feet, she was beautiful. Her face shone with love and was aglitter with the finest ocean diamond dust. Long, black ringlets curled down her back and over her shoulders, woven with glowing anemone silk threaded with gems and ancient coins gathered from a thousand years of sunken treasure. A ball gown wrapped around her that shimmered and rustled in colours that he had never before seen. Afterwards, he could only describe it as how he would feel if he took mint tea in a mother-of-pearl shell after spinning on a round-about. She wore coral flower perfume, which if you have never smelt, makes you quite silly with happiness. Marguerite held out her hand to the Captain.

"Happy birthday, Captain, our very special Captain," said she.

"Let's have ourselves one fat hooly!" shouted Big Mac from somewhere among the crowd.

And the whole ship immediately echoed with laughter, cheers and shouts, and with that Captain Antonio took Marguerite's hand and began to dance to the music of stars and light, and ocean and love. Violins set the tune, the feet of hearty sailors stamped a beat, and throughout that wonderful night each and every guest spun and twirled, and laughed, and ate and drank and were truly merry.

The Chocolate Ambassador and his wife waltzed gracefully, while the sailors of Bear de Sol sang shanties and clinked tankards of nutty ale. The Great Ocean King joked heartily with Jacques and the '*Aquila Spice*' crew. Max did his level best to steal as many pickled pearls for Roly as he dared, while Star and Sea danced the jig. La Chocolat, who looked truly beautiful and seemed very grown up with her black-golden hair wound into a lovely chignon and wearing one of Marguerite's ball gowns, managed to sneak in a few dances of her own with all the best-looking sailors. Land had to keep a sharp eye out as more than one of those sailors lost their heart to her.

As the morning dawned pink and golden and new, Captain Antonio sat on the deck of his fine schooner amongst all of his favourite people and gazed across at '*Aquila Spice*'.

He reflected on all of his adventures and came to one conclusion.

The people that his adventures had brought, made his life so full of joy that he could not imagine a time before his heart was opened and love had poured right in. And if more adventures were out there to be had, then by jove!

With a slap on his thigh and a tip of his hat, he was up for them all!

The End